FRASER DINGO

by Jill Morris
illustrated by Sharon Dye

Greater Glider Productions Maleny Queensland Australia

Special thanks to Sue Olsson, Department of Environment Queensland;
to Rod Hobson and all Fraser Island rangers; to Dr Laurie Corbett;
and to Kingfisher Bay Resort.

First published August 1998
by Greater Glider Productions, 330 Reesville Rd, Maleny, Queensland
typeset by Range Rose, Maleny, Queensland
designed by Lynne Muir, Melbourne, Victoria
printed & bound by Fergies, Hamilton, Queensland

National Library of Australia Cataloguing-in-Publication data

Morris, Jill, 1936- .
 Fraser dingo.

 ISBN 0 947304 39 8.

 1. Dingo - Queensland - Fraser Island. I. Dye, Sharon. II.
 Title.

599.77209432

CONTENTS

SWISH! The dingo pup's ears pricked at the sound of
movement down by the lake. He stopped chewing on a lump
of leather which had once been a shoe and froze to listen,
while the other pups played their fighting game.

Perhaps a LongLegs was approaching? His mother said a
LongLegs could kill a pup with one blow. A flash of orange
fur told ShortSocks that his mother was on her way back to
the den. He nosed forward, to be first to claim the food she
had brought.

SoftFace was proud of the pup who came to greet her.
From birth he had pushed the others out of the way to suckle.
'When you are older I will take you to see the LongLegs,' she
told him. 'Your father ScarFace will take you hunting for
bandicoot. But food is easier to find in the LongLegs' tents.'

SoftFace's first litter had all been killed in the den by the Lake
Pack's leading female. Now she was the leader, her pups
would be looked after by the whole pack. ShortSocks would
grow up to be a fierce fighter.

To the north along the beach, in a hidden den behind the Big Dune, an older female called WhiteLegs whelped four pups. WhiteLegs was respected by her pack. Her son from three seasons ago, HighWhiteRightSock, had grown to be chief fighter.

Life was good on the beach. The LongLegs with poles who threw lines into the sea and pulled out fish stored their catch in buckets. The Beach Pack were always ready, when the LongLegs turned their backs, to dart and grab a squirming fish. When the LongLegs cut up the fish and buried the offal in shallow holes in the sand, the dingoes dug it up again.

There was always time for a roll and shake in the warm channel of water left by the sea.

The Beach Pack kept constant guard over their territory, alert for the approach of other packs.

The Headland Pack padded silently along secret trails over the hills behind the Big Dune, looking for food. When the Headland Pack YOWL-ed a challenge fom the Big Dune, the Beach Pack answered back loudly to show their strength.

The Beach Pack and the Headland Pack were at war.

ShortSocks had grown tall and strong. He was almost ready to leave his pack to find his own territory. His mother had mentioned the Big Creek, where she had been whelped.

ShortSocks was curious about the Big Creek. One damp afternoon, he strayed into the territory of the Big Creek Pack, unaware of the danger.

ShortSocks was seen by the leading pair of the Big Creek Pack. They determined to kill him. ShortSocks put up a good fight but the older male attacked again and again. The older male and female savaged his throat, his chest, his stomach and his back.

ShortSocks tried not to die. He staggered to his feet - then fell again. The female put her snout close to his. He was still breathing! Her mate tore at the young throat until ShortSocks lay still and even his tail had stopped twitching.

Their territory was safe.

As night fell, ScarFace took the teenage pups of the Lake Pack
out along a sandy road between giant trees to teach them to
hunt for bandicoot, antechinus and rat.

They had so much to learn.

On the night the Headland Pack attacked the Beach Pack, WhiteLegs hid her pups in long grass, but she and her pups were all killed. HighWhiteRightSock also died, defending his pack's territory.

After the battle, the new pack leader, CurvedWhiteSock, became excited with his new power. He began to threaten the LongLegs, becoming more daring with each attack.

Eventually he was trapped by the LongLegs, put into a cage and taken away to be destroyed. His pack followed the truck down the road, yowling.

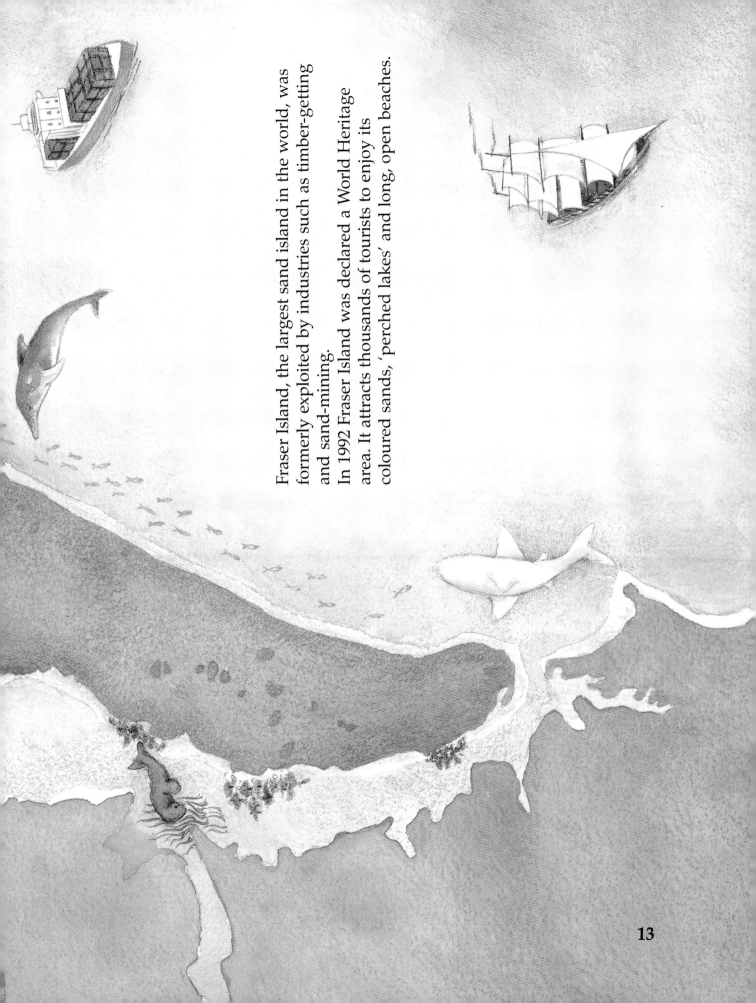

Fraser Island, the largest sand island in the world, was formerly exploited by industries such as timber-getting and sand-mining.

In 1992 Fraser Island was declared a World Heritage area. It attracts thousands of tourists to enjoy its coloured sands, 'perched lakes' and long, open beaches.

DON'T FEED THE DINGOES! (A Play)

CAST: MUM, DAD, BEN, KATY, UNCLE, AUNT,
              DINGO *(looks hungry but does not speak)*
SCENE: PORTABLE BARBECUE ABOVE A LAKE.
              (Ben is offering a scrap to Dingo)

MUM: Ben - don't feed the dingoes!

BEN: It's just fat off the meat. Where else can I put it?

MUM: In the bin, Ben.

BEN: It's too far away and I'm too hot. Here, Dingo...

MUM: Don't feed the dingoes!

BEN: But it's looking at me. It's hungry.

AUNT: It's so thin, poor thing!

MUM: They're naturally skinny, like greyhounds.

BEN: Mum! What else can I do with it?

KATY: You could bury it.

BEN: The dingoes'd dig it up again, stupid!

KATY: But what can they eat?

DAD: Berries. Bandicoots. Rats.

BEN: Gross!

KATY: Yuk!

MUM: Ben, come and get your lunch.

BEN: Smells good.

KATY: Sorry, Dingo. You can't have any.

BEN: Sausages. Steak. Eggs. Bacon. Yum! Mum - Uncle Bob
              threw the eggshells and bacon rinds in the sand.

UNCLE: The dingoes'll clean that up.

BEN: No, Uncle Bob. We're not supposed to feed them.

UNCLE: Rubbish. Look how scrawny they are!

AUNT: That's what I said.

UNCLE: Mm. Great steak.

KATY: This one's just a baby. It's so cute.

MUM: Katy! Stay close to us. Come and eat your lunch.

KATY: I'm not hungry. Come and play with me, Dingo.
              (She goes down to lake) AAGH! Mum - that dingo bit me!

MUM: Bad Dingo! Shoo! Bad dog!

UNCLE: Those dingoes are dangerous. Should be shot.

BEN: The dingo didn't do anything wrong, Uncle Bob. We did.

Finding Food

Despite the diversity of wildlife on Fraser Island, the Dingoes are specialist eaters, concentrating on small mammals such as rats, antechinuses, bandicoots and other small mammals, as well as fish, insects and berries. They also like cooked foods such as chicken and will readily gather people's food scraps.

Carpet Python

Swamp Wallaby

Short-beaked Echidna

tailor

This unnatural diet can make them aggressive to humans and put both the humans and the dingoes in danger.

Many objects left by humans are also regarded by the dingoes as 'food': packages and plastic bags which have contained food; hats, shoes, dirty clothes, bedding, dirty nappies, used tissues, bandaids, bandages and toilet paper; and human excrement.

Northern Brown Bandicoot

Fawn-footed Melomys

Scarlet Honeyeater

Bar-shouldered Dove

Short-tailed Shearwater

NOT TO SCALE

Lace Monitor

Yellow-footed Antechinus

Growing in Sand

On Fraser Island, a wide range of
plants from giant trees to tiny
wildflowers grow in sand,
supporting a variety of wildlife.
Many of the plants provided food
for the Aboriginal people of the
Butchulla (or Badtjala) group, who
cared for the island for centuries
before the arrival of European
settlers.

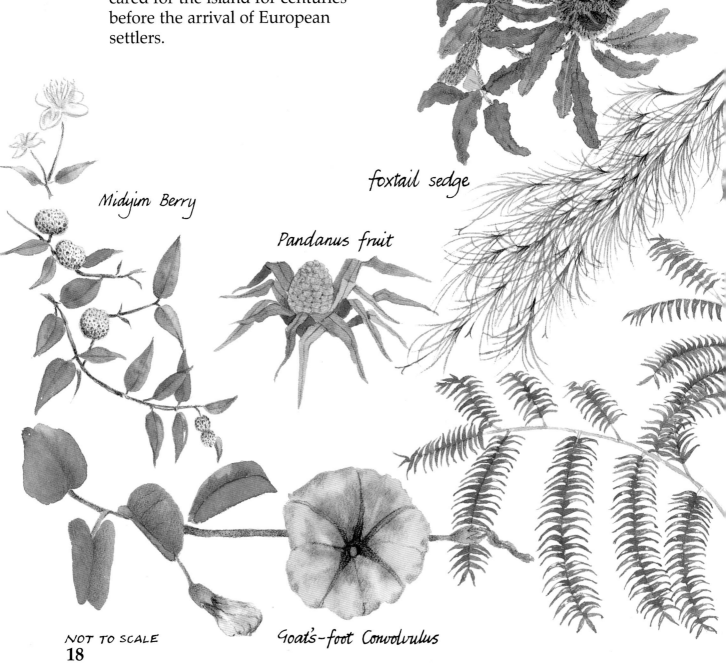

Banksia

Midjim Berry

foxtail sedge

Pandanus fruit

Goat's-foot Convolvulus

NOT TO SCALE

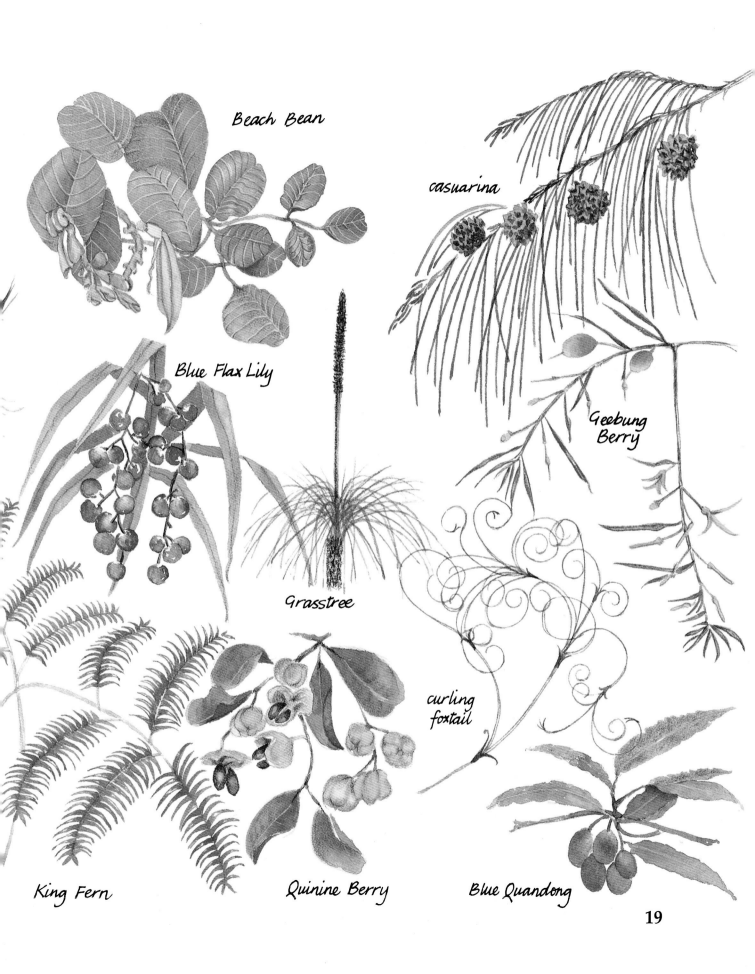

Beach Bean

casuarina

Blue Flax Lily

Grasstree

Geebung Berry

curling foxtail

King Fern

Quinine Berry

Blue Quandong

19

Osprey

White-bellied Sea-eagle

Curlew Sandpiper

Pied Oystercatcher

dart

bluebottle

NOT TO SCALE

20

Brahminy Kite

Eastern Curlew

Yellow-bellied Seasnake

blubber

Where Land Meets Sea

The upper and lower sand dunes of Fraser Island and the beachfront above the tidemark are visited by many species of birds, which vary according to the season.

True Dingo Tales

Dingoes don't like putting their snouts under water. A goanna pursued by dingoes will go deep into a lake to escape.

In the north of Fraser Island, a pack of dingoes were hunting a Swamp Wallaby by herding it into the sea. The teenage dingoes in charge of the beach section of the hunt were butted for their carelessness when the Swamp Wallaby disappeared. Human observers thought it had been taken by a shark!

A group of fishermen left their Christmas turkey cooking in a camp oven over coals while they went off to the beach. They were horrified to see their Christmas dinner disappearing over the sand dunes in the mouth of a dingo.

A sleeping man lying on the bench of a picnic table after lunch woke suddenly when a dingo snatched his leather hat. In the middle of the night a dingo pulled a feather pillow from under the head of a sleeping woman in a beachside tent.

Dingoes have carried off dirty nappies, sleeping bags, and even a pack full of saucepans. They find it easy to open eskies. Clever campers keep their food in locked boxes.

A dingo bitch followed a ranger, trying to attract his attention, to let him know that her pup was caught in a craypot. The ranger followed the dingo to the 'potted' pup and set it free.

Fraser Island Dingoes

The Australian Dingo *Canis lupus dingo* belongs to the same family as the Wolf.

Scientists studying fossils believe that the Dingo came to Australia from Asia about 4 000 years ago.

Dingoes are different from the domestic dogs which people keep as pets. They have narrower, longer snouts, bigger ear bones and different tooth structure. They are wild animals.

Dingoes are found in most parts of Australia except Tasmania.

The dingoes of Fraser Island (about 200 animals) are perhaps the purest breed of Australian dingoes as they have had less exposure than mainland animals to inter-breeding with other dogs. An individual animal can be identified by its 'socks' (white marks on legs), tip of the tail and colour of fur (white facial fur in older dogs, dark markings on the back in younger dogs); scars on face and head; chewed ear; or limp.

For the survival of Fraser Island dingoes, it is vital that they have no interaction with humans. Feeding the dingoes, and leaving food or other objects regarded as food by dingoes, has led to some attack situations for humans and caused individual dingoes to be destroyed.